IMAGINE

Alison Lester

For Rich and Bee

Houghton Mifflin Company

Boston

Library of Congress Cataloging-in-Publication Data

Lester, Alison.
    Imagine/Alison Lester. — 1st American ed.
    p. cm.
Summary: Invites the reader to imagine what it
would be like to live in various locations, such as
a house, a jungle, and an icecap, and meet the
animals that live there.
    HC ISBN 0-395-53753-3   PA ISBN 0-395-66953-7
    [1. Imagination — Fiction. 2. Animals — Fiction.
    3. Stories in rhyme.]   I. Title.
PZ8.3.L54935Im 1990
[E] — dc20   89 29228
                             CIP
                             AC

Copyright © 1989 by Alison Lester
First American edition 1990
Originally published in Australia in 1989 by Allen
& Unwin Australia Pty Ltd.

Printed in Singapore
TWP 10 9 8 7 6 5 4 3 2 1

IMAGINE

Imagine
if we were
deep in the jungle
where butterflies drift
and jaguars prowl
where parakeets squawk
and wild monkeys howl . . .

∎

Imagine
if we were
like fish in the ocean
where anemones wave
and hammerheads glide
where seahorses rock
and hermit crabs hide . . .

■

scorpion-fish • coral • snapper • sea-cucumber • sea-urchin • cowrie • parrotfish • nudibranch • spe

nautilus • lamprey • cowrie • jellyfish • seahorse • octopus • lobster • coral

• white pointer shark • dolphin • turtle • sea-dragon • puffer fish • crab • squid • scallop • wrasse •

ale • hermit crab • sawfish • butterfly fish • giant clam • angelfish • angler fish • sea-snake • sponge •

tusk fish • hammerhead shark • prawn • starfish • moray eel • stingray

fish • trumpet-fish • swordfish • flounder • moorish idol • limpet • clownfish • anemone • oyster

Imagine
if we were
crossing the icecap
where penguins toboggan
and arctic hares dash
where caribou snort
and killer whales crash . . .

∎

humpback whale • narwhal • arctic dolphin • adelie penguin • arctic hare

Imagine
if we were
out in the country
where horses gallop
and cattle graze
where turkeys gobble
and sheepdogs laze . . .

■

Imagine
if we were
surrounded by monsters
where pteranodons swoop
and triceratops smash
where stegosaurs stomp
and tyrannosaurs gnash . . .

■

Imagine
if we were
away on safari
where crocodiles lurk
and antelope feed
where leopards attack
and zebras stampede . . .

■

n • crocodile • rhinoceros • colobus monkey • warthog • zebra • jackal • baboon • ibex • impala

aardvark • flamingo • vulture • crowned crane • leopard • okapi • dik-dik

pi • dik-dik • chimpanzee • gazelle • ostrich • leopard • bushbaby • buffalo • elephant • cheetah

Imagine
if we were
alone in Australia
where bandicoots nibble
and wallabies jump
where wombats dig burrows
and kangaroos thump . . .

■

Imagine
if we had
our own little house
with a cat on the bed
a rug on the floor
a light in the night
and a dog at the door . . .

■

Imagine . . .

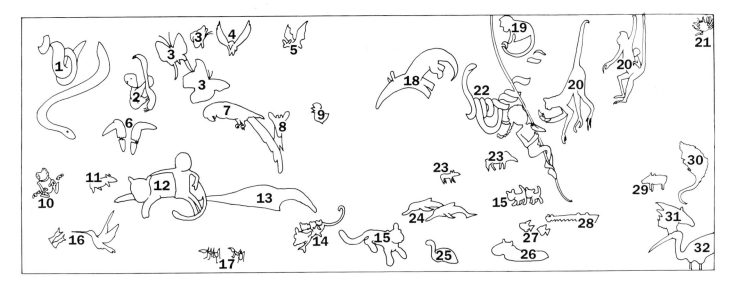

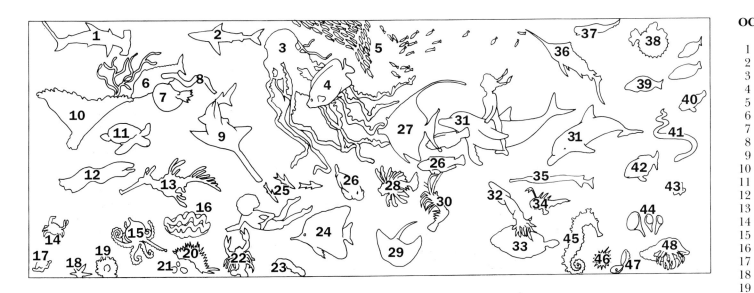

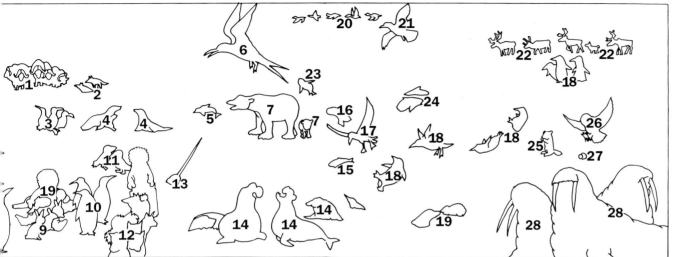

ICECAP

1	musk ox	15	herring
2	arctic wolf	16	beluga whale
3	guillemot	17	albatross
4	sea lion	18	adelie penguin
5	arctic dolphin	19	harp seal
6	arctic tern	20	snow goose
7	polar bear	21	kittiwake
8	loon	22	caribou
9	arctic hare	23	humpback whale
10	emperor penguin	24	killer whale
11	puffin	25	arctic squirrel
12	husky	26	snowy owl
13	narwhal	27	lemming
14	elephant seal	28	walrus

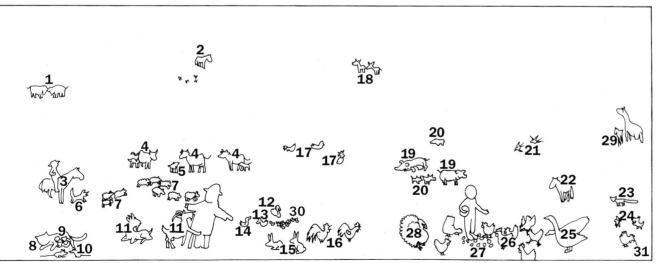

FARM

1	bull	17	cockatoo
2	draughthorse	18	donkey
3	stockhorse	19	pig
4	cow	20	piglet
5	calf	21	swallow
6	sheepdog	22	pony
7	sheep	23	fox
8	cat	24	puppy
9	kitten	25	goose
10	mouse	26	hen
11	goat	27	chick
12	swan	28	turkey
13	duck	29	foal
14	drake	30	duckling
15	rabbit	31	worm
16	rooster		

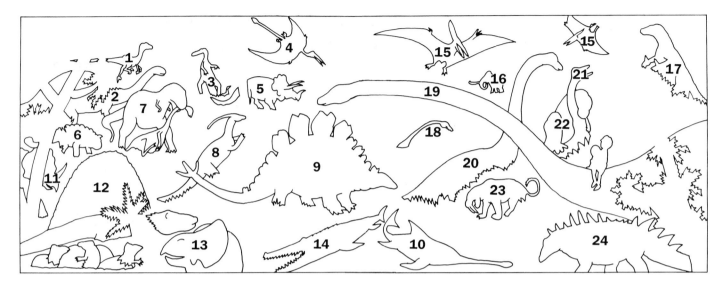

DINOSAUR SWAMP

1	deinonychus	13	protoceratops
2	brontosaurus	14	metriorhynch
3	anatosaurus	15	pteranodon
4	rhamphorhynchus	16	woolly mamm
5	triceratops	17	iguanodon
6	ankylosaurus	18	elasmosaurus
7	tyrannosaurus	19	diplodocus
8	parasaurolophus	20	brachiosaurus
9	stegosaurus	21	corythosaurus
10	ichthyosaurus	22	allosaurus
11	monoclonius	23	sabre-toothed
12	dimetrodon	24	polacanthus

AFRICAN PLAIN

1	vulture	17	lion
2	leopard	18	zebra
3	giraffe	19	wildebeest
4	gazelle	20	impala
5	okapi	21	antelope
6	buffalo	22	elephant
7	orynx	23	dik-dik
8	ibex	24	ostrich
9	baboon	25	cheetah
10	crowned crane	26	warthog
11	hippopotamus	27	hyena
12	rhinoceros	28	chimpanzee
13	crocodile	29	bush baby
14	mandrill	30	flamingo
15	aardvark	31	colobus monk
16	jackal	32	gorilla

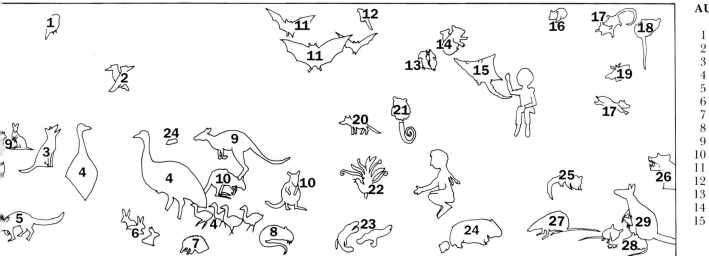

AUSTRALIAN BUSH

1	mopoke	16	tiger quoll
2	kookaburra	17	sugar glider
3	dingo	18	pigmy possum
4	emu	19	emperor gum moth
5	numbat	20	tasmanian tiger
6	rabbit	21	ringtail possum
7	echidna	22	lyrebird
8	water-rat	23	platypus
9	kangaroo	24	wombat
10	wallaby	25	brushtail possum
11	flying fox	26	tasmanian devil
12	tawny frogmouth	27	bandicoot
13	cockatoo	28	marsupial mouse
14	koala	29	pademelon
15	feather-tail glider		